Soldier Sam and Trooper Ted

The son of a diplomat, John Ryan spent his early childhood in places like Turkey and Morocco. After wartime service in Burma, he studied art in Regent Street and then taught at Harrow School. He originally created Captain Pugwash and other characters for *Eagle Magazine* and later developed them for picture books and TV films.

John Ryan now lives in Rye, Sussex, with his wife Priscilla, Captain Pugwash and other assorted characters. He continues to work hard on books, theatre design, playwrighting and the occasional painting.

AV

58/C

C7068400 99

First published 1994 by Pan Macmillan Children's Books
a division of Pan Macmillan Publishers Limited
Cavaye Place London SW10 9PG
and Basingstoke

Associated companies throughout the world

ISBN 0 333 59258 1

9 8 7 6 5 4 3 2 1

A CIP catalogue record for this book is available from
the British Library

Soldier Sam
and
Trooper Ted

The Battle That Never Was

John Ryan

PAN MACMILLAN
CHILDRENS BOOKS

Chapter One

There was once a soldier called Sam. He was short and fat. He was no good at all at looking smart or marching in time or shooting straight, or indeed doing any of the things that soldiers are supposed to be good at.

In fact, he was so useless all round that
when a war broke out between his
country and the one next door . . .

. . . he was given the job of looking after
an officer, whose name was Lieutenant
Nibs.

Sam was
supposed
to polish
his boots,

keep his
uniform
pressed and
tidy,

wash his
socks,
and make
his bed.

He wasn't much good at that either but
it didn't matter because Lieutenant Nibs,
whom everybody called "Nibbles" behind
his back, couldn't get anyone else to look
after him anyway.

One fine summer
morning, General
Bingleburg-Botch,
who commanded
the Regiment,
sent for Lieutenant
Nibs and said,
"Nibs! There's
a war on, y'know!
It's time we
had a battle!
Troops are gettin' far too comfortable
lyin' about and enjoying themselves!
And it's time I had a few more medals
to show how important I am."

"*I* shall lead you nowhere!
I have the Commander-in-Chief comin'
to dinner with me this evenin'.
This is *your* battle, Nibs! See to it!"

"Yes, General.
Of course,
General," said
Lieutenant Nibs, and he saluted
and went back to his tent to find Sam.

"Sam" said he, "there's
going to be a battle."

"Oh, aye, sir,"
answered Sam.
"Why's that?
And who against,
sir?"
He didn't like the
idea of a battle
one little bit.

"Yes, General!
Certainly, General.
At once, General,"
answered the Lieutenant.

"But – er – what sort
of battle had you in
mind, and – er – who
shall we fight
it against?"
"Use your eyes, Nibs!" snorted the
General. "There's a perfectly good
enemy sittin' on that hill over there!

"They're wearin'
blue uniforms,
and since ours are
red, they must
be enemies."
"Why, of course, sir.
How stupid of me,"
said Nibs. "And
at what time,
may I ask,
will it please
you to lead
us into action?"
"Action! . . . Me lead
it! Certainly not!" roared the General.

"Why? Because the General says so, of course! And who against? Those fellas on that hill over there. They've got blue uniforms, which means they must be our enemies because we've got red uniforms, which is what all proper soldiers ought to wear. Understand?"

"Yes, sir!" said Sam, though he didn't understand at all. "First thing is to find out all about the enemy," continued Lieutenant Nibs.

"That means sending out a scout. A brave man, Sam! Someone who won't mind giving his life if needs be . . .

. . . for me and the General." "Can't think of nobody like that, sir," said Sam.

"I can," replied the Lieutenant.
"You, Sam. To tell the truth, you're about the only soldier who wouldn't be missed if he didn't come back.

"Off you go! And make sure nobody can see you. Disguise yourself as a bush or something. Good luck!"

"It'll take more than luck to get
me out of this one," thought Sam.
"I'm sure to get shot if
I go, and I'll probably
get shot if
I don't!"

So he collected lots of branches,
leaves and flowers and did
his best to look like a bush.

Chapter Two

Sam set out towards the enemy hill.

It was a lovely day. Birds sang, bees
buzzed, and wild flowers bloomed on
every side.

All that Soldier Sam wanted to do was to sit down and enjoy a little snooze in the sunshine.

He was just thinking how much nicer
that would be than crawling through the
countryside pretending to be a large bush . . .

. . . when he heard a loud crashing noise
in front of him. He was very surprised
to see that the noise was made by an odd -
looking tree . . .

. . . which seemed to be coming towards him.

Then he tripped up
and fell flat on the ground.
Behind it . . .

. . . stood
another
soldier.
He was tall
and rather thin.
Like Sam, he
carried a big
gun in his
hand.
And he was
wearing a
blue uniform!

Sam scrambled to his feet.

"Hands up!" he shouted.

"Hands up!" shouted the other soldier. So they both put their hands up . . .

"Drop your gun!" cried Sam.

"You drop yours!" shouted the other.
And they both dropped their guns, and
stood looking at each other.
"You've got a RED uniform," said
the tall soldier. "That means you must be
an enemy!"
"So must you! Yours is BLUE,"
replied Sam.

"In that case," said the stranger, "we ought to shoot each other."

"But that would be silly," Sam said. "My mum and dad would be very upset if anything happened to me. And you don't look like an enemy."

"Nor do you. And I rather like
your red uniform. Let's shake hands
and be friends instead. My name's Ted,
Trooper Ted."

So the two soldiers shook hands and sat
in the shade of a real tree and Ted told
Sam his side of the story.
"It's like this," he began.

"There's this officer
I look after, his
name's Rott –
Tommy Rott we call him, and this
morning our General Rumbletum calls
my officer and says it's time we had a
battle, because it's time he got a few
more medals to keep up with all the
other generals, only we've got to do
the fighting.

"So Lieutenant Rott calls me and says there's going to be a battle,

And I've got to go and be a scout and find out all about the enemy . . . that's you . . .

So I disguises meself as a tree, so as not to be spotted . . . and here I am!"

"I seem to have heard all this before somewhere," said Sam. "But it's much more fun sitting here chatting than killing each other."

"Agreed," said Trooper Ted.

"Let's swap jackets. Then nobody will know which side we're supposed to be on."

They looked
a bit odd, because
Sam's wide one
flopped over Ted's
shoulders and Ted's
narrow one didn't
fit Sam at all.
But now they
both had red and
blue uniforms.
"I tell you what,"
said Sam . . .
"I'm hungry!"

"There's a farmhouse
over there," said
Ted, pointing.
"Let's go and see
if we can get
something to eat . . . "

It was very quiet when they got to
the farm. The animals were all shut
in their sheds and
all the doors were locked.

Ted knocked on the front door.
"Go away!" called a girl's voice from
inside. "We don't want any soldiers here!"
Ted knocked again,
louder.

A window opened upstairs.
"Off with you!"
shouted another
girl's voice.
"We don't want
any of your
silly fighting
neither."

"It's all right. We're friends,"
called Sam. "We
don't want to
fight anybody."

"Only we're hungry," added Ted.
"Can you sell us something to eat?"

Both girls came to the front door.
They took a closer peep through
the keyhole.

They liked the look of Sam and Ted.
They both had kind faces.
They didn't look warlike at all.

They opened the door.
"Come in," they said. "Only
leave those stupid guns outside."

So Soldier Sam and Trooper Ted went in.
Ted banged his head on the low door.

"You'll soon get used to that," said the
taller of the two girls.
"I do it all the time!
My name's Peg . . . "

"And I'm Meg," said the other,
who was shortish and plumpish.
"Make yourselves at home."

Then the soldiers sat down, and
the girls brought bread and butter,
cheese, milk and honey,
and Sam and Ted told Meg and Peg
all about themselves and their generals.

Chapter Three

"We're supposed to be enemy scouts,"
said Sam, "finding out about each other
so that there can be a big battle
this evening."

"Only there's going to be terrible
trouble when they find out that we've
become friends, and we're not going back.
So they won't be able to have their
battle after all," said Ted.

"I know," said Meg, "why don't we have a pretend battle instead? Then everybody would be happy."

"But how?" asked Ted.

"Well," explained Peg, "the last time there was a battle near here, some soldiers brought loads of boxes of ammunition to the farm. Then they all took fright and ran away. The boxes are still here, hundreds of them, in the barn."

The girls
took Sam and
Ted out and
showed them.

"Bullets," said Sam, opening one of the boxes. "Bombs," said Ted, "and gunpowder." And between them they worked out a plan.

First they chose
a pair of haystacks
a long way away
from the farm

Then they loaded all
the bullets and
bombs on to
a farm
waggon . . .

. . . and took them
into the field.

They unloaded everything between
the haystacks.
Then, as darkness fell . . .

. . . they set fire to the hay

and as they rushed back to the farm . . .

the "battle" began.

And what a battle it was!

Thousands of bullets and bombs
exploded with a fearful din,

And for his part General Rumbletum was also watching the battle in between courses.

"That's what I like to hear," said he, to his guest. "Nothing like a bit of action to keep the lads happy . . . If you ask me, I deserve a medal or two . . ."

In the morning, General Botch sent
for Lieutenant Nibs.

"Sounds like a splendid fight you had
last night, Nibs," said he. "Glorious
victory, eh? Lose many men?"

"Well, er . . . yes, sir . . . I mean, no, sir,
um . . . thank you, sir . . . I'll find out,
sir," said Nibs.

He had hidden under his bed the moment
he heard the sounds of battle, so he hadn't
the faintest idea what had really happened,
or who had won, or anything . . .

And when he got his men out on
parade to check the numbers,
he found all present
and correct, except
for Soldier Sam.

"Only one
man missing,
sir," he reported to
the General. "Fella called Sam.
And *he* wasn't much good to anyone
anyway!"
"Good show," said General Botch.

"Now we can all go home, and I can get my medals and retire, and you, Nibs, can become a general in my place."

And exactly the same thing happened with Trooper Ted's Army, and Lieutenant Rott and General Rumbletum.

Back on the farm, Sam and Ted and
Meg and Peg watched the two armies
setting out for home.

Then they cleaned up the mess left by
the battle.

"It was hard work, but it was worth it," said Sam. "Aye, that it was," said Ted.

"Talking of hard work, how about staying on and helping us run the farm?" asked Peg.

"Yes, we could do with a hand," said Meg. "Suits me," said Sam. "Me too," agreed Ted. So they did . . .

and the story ended well for everyone.

The two generals got so many medals that, as they got older, they could hardly carry the weight. So they retired to their clubs . . .

Blah blah!

Blah Blah!

. . . and spent their days telling everybody about their great victories.

The two lieutenants became generals . . .

. . . and down on the farm, Sam
married Peg and Meg
married Ted.

Soon there were quite a lot of
little Megs and Sams and Pegs and Teds.

They were all very happy . . .

It's a pity all battles
don't end like that.